FIRST CHAPTER BOOKS

TIME CHRONICLES

READ WITH
Biff,
Chip &
Kipper

Beyond
the Door

Written by Roderick Hunt
and illustrated by Alex Brychta

OXFORD

Before reading

- Read the back cover text and page 4. What do you think the children will find beyond the door?
- Look at the diagram on page 5. What sort of place do you think the Time Vault might be?

After reading

- Look at the illustration on page 28 and the information on page 40. Why is it so important for Mortlock to get the TimeWeb working?
- What do you think is going to happen next, after the end of this story?

Book quiz

1 What is the name of Mortlock's ancient means of time travel?
   a The TimeWeb
   b The Circularium
   c The Viran
2 What are Virans made of?
3 How does Mortlock make the Circularium start spinning?

See p45 for the book quiz answers!

The story so far...

At the school fair Nadim buys the box that once had the magic key inside it. When a sinister man tries to get it, Mr Mortlock, the school caretaker, prevents him.

Who is Mr Mortlock? Why does he call the man "the enemy", and why is the box so important? And what will happen when the children run through the door that suddenly appears in the landscape?

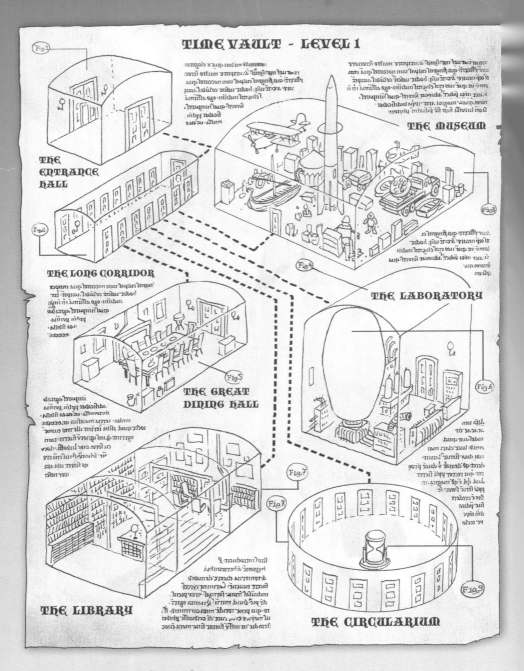

TIME VAULT - LEVEL 1

Map of the Time Vault [Level 1]

"... the Time Vault is a place that exists outside time..."

Theodore Mortlock – Time Guardian

Chapter 1

What were the children thinking as they ran through the door? Their minds were racing.

How could a man disappear in a shower of sparks before their eyes? Was he even human?

Wilma checked that everyone had made it. "We're all safe! And Floppy too. Thank goodness!" she breathed.

Nadim still held the box that the man had tried to snatch from them. "Where are we, and what do we do now?" he asked.

They were in an empty hallway with doors leading off it.

"Let's try the first door," said Chip nervously.

They pushed the door open and stepped into a vast room full of exhibits on display.

"It's like a museum," gasped Kipper.

Everything looked strangely familiar – a robot, a Viking ship and a lorry with a huge mirror on the back.

In the centre of the room was a rocket ship. From the ceiling hung a biplane with a yellow body and blue wings.

Dresses and costumes hung on racks round the walls.

"This is amazing," gasped Biff. "These are from adventures we had with the magic key when we were younger."

"This robot was in Storm Castle," cried Nadim.

"The biplane was in the Blue Eye adventure," said Wilf, "and there's the rainbow machine."

"There's something weird about all this," said Biff. "Why are these things in here? I don't understand it."

Neena said what they were all thinking.

"Magic key adventures were often scary, but they were fun. When the key glowed, we came back. This is different. What if something has gone wrong?"

"Well, it must have something to do with this old box," said Nadim.

"We found the magic key in the box," said Kipper. "That man wanted the box, but Mr Mortlock zapped him."

"So the horrid man, this box, Mr Mortlock and the magic key are all connected in some way," said Nadim. "But how?"

"Let's go back to the hallway and try another door," suggested Wilf.

Chapter 2

As they went back to the hallway, Floppy growled. A door was opening. It was the door they had come through from the park.

The children gasped. Mr Mortlock was running through the doorway. There was a flash of light and the door slammed shut.

But it was not Mr Mortlock, it was an old man. He had long, white hair. His skin was leathery and lined. He smiled at them kindly, his blue eyes looking wise but sad.

"Who are you?" gasped Wilma. "You look like Mr Mortlock, our school caretaker, only much older."

"I am a Time Guardian. My name is Mortlock," the old man replied. "We are in the Time Vault. Outside here, I turn into Mr Mortlock, the school caretaker. I have worked at your school for many years to protect you from danger."

"Danger?" exclaimed Nadim. "Is it to do with the man who exploded in the park? But he wasn't a man at all, was he? Why was he so keen to get his hands on this box?"

"You are right," said Mortlock. "The man was not a human. All this has to do with the box you are holding, Nadim."

Kipper remembered the exhibits on display in the other room. "So you are behind the magic key adventures?" he said.

"Yes. They were a test," said Mortlock, "and you were resourceful, brave and clever. I could not have hoped for more."

Biff was angry. "A test for what? Magic key adventures were exciting. What happened today was horrible."

Mortlock held up his hand. "I am sorry. This must be quite a shock for you all, but I need your help. Come with me. What I have to show you will make everything clear."

Chapter 3

Mortlock led them into a laboratory. A huge vat made of thick glass was connected to a tangle of tubes and wires. Inside it was an inky darkness, blacker than anything the children had ever seen before.

Flashes and sparks shot through the blackness like lightning in a storm.

"In this vat, is the enemy," said Mortlock. "Virans!"

Kipper felt the hair rise up on the back of his neck.

"The man you met today was a Viran," Mortlock went on. "He was not human, he was made of the dark energy you see in here. The Virans' aim is to destroy history and bring about darkness and confusion. As a Time Guardian, I protect time by seeking out Virans and trapping them. What you see inside this vat is more terrible than you can imagine. It cannot be destroyed, it has to be trapped and must never escape."

The children shuddered. An icy chill ran through them. Floppy looked at the dark vessel, lifted his head and howled.

"Let's not stay here," said Mortlock.

Chapter 4

Mortlock took them to a huge library. It had shelves of books that went up to the tall ceiling. The books were all bound in polished leather. Some did not have titles, they had a date on the spine with some strange letters and symbols. Along a wall were cabinets with hundreds of tiny drawers.

A log fire burned cosily at the far end of the room. The children sat on comfortable leather chairs and Floppy lay on the thick carpet in front of the fire and fell asleep. Mortlock sank into a chair, wiped his forehead with a handkerchief, leaned forward, and began.

"You are my only hope," Mortlock said. "I need you to go on a mission. It will be difficult and dangerous. I want you to travel back in time and bring back the TimeWeb. We have the box already but there are three more parts that must be brought here."

"What is the TimeWeb?" asked Neena.

"It is an ancient machine. It acts like an eye looking into the past. It tells us where the Virans are attacking time. Without it, we cannot look back in history to see where they are. We need the TimeWeb so we can travel back in time to stop them. However, if they get hold of any part of the TimeWeb before us, we can never defeat them."

Mortlock's pale eyes burned into them.

"And today, as you saw, a Viran almost succeeded."

Nadim gulped. He held out the old box which he had not let out of his sight. "So this is part of the TimeWeb?" he gasped.

"That's right," said Mortlock.

Chapter 5

From a chest, Mortlock took out a diagram. "The TimeWeb looks like this. See, it has four parts. The Hub is a bit like the hard drive of a computer, the Matrix is like the keyboard and the Cell gives the TimeWeb its power. The old box is the case which connects it all together."

"But how does it work?" asked Kipper.

"It's like a very strange and ancient computer," explained Mortlock. "It links you to the past, rather like a computer links you to the internet."

"So when the Virans attack the past and try to change it, the TimeWeb can tell you where they are," suggested Neena. "No wonder the Virans want to get hold of it."

"But we've had the box ever since we found the magic key," said Biff. "So it's been lost for years. If it's so important, why didn't you look after it?"

Mortlock smiled. "Ah, not lost! It was hidden. I can think of no safer place than in your hands. The other parts of the TimeWeb are hidden in history. Your task will be to find them."

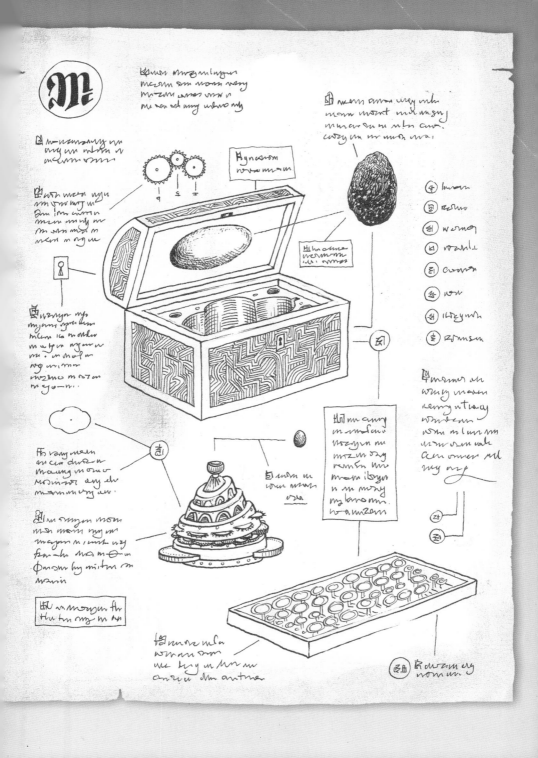

"If we go on this mission to bring back these parts, how will we know where to look?" Nadim asked doubtfully.

"And how dangerous will it be?" asked Kipper. "Will we meet Virans?"

"You will know where to look when you get there," said Mortlock. "But the Virans are getting close. You may have to outwit them."

"Do the Virans all look the same?" asked Neena. She shuddered when she thought of the terrible man they had met that afternoon.

"No," replied Mortlock gravely, "most of them look like ordinary people. But Virans can give off a feeling of coldness and darkness, and ..."

"Like that man did," cried Kipper.

As the oldest, Wilma felt responsible, so she spoke for all of them. "I think we're all agreed to go," she said. They all nodded.

"Then every second is precious," said Mortlock. He jumped to his feet and ran from the library. The children followed.

As the library door banged shut, Floppy opened one eye, yawned and went back to sleep.

Chapter 6

The children rushed after Mortlock. He led them along winding passages, down stairs and then down a flight of stone steps. As they went deeper, the steps grew narrow and uneven. The air smelled damp and earthy, as if they were in some ancient vault deep underground.

At last they came to a heavy wooden door. Mortlock pushed it open, and beckoned them through.

It was a circular room with doors evenly spaced round it. Each door had a key in it. In the centre of the room was a huge hourglass, almost as tall as Kipper. "This is the Circularium," announced Mortlock, "an ancient means of time travel."

"It will choose which of you will go, and where in time you will travel. As there are three parts of the TimeWeb still to get, only three doors will work."

Mortlock took the box that Nadim was still holding. He told each of them to choose a door, then he flipped the hourglass upside down.

At once, tiny specks of bright light began to flow into the lower chamber of the hourglass.

The Circularium began to spin. The doors seemed to merge into one. Then the spinning stopped.

Biff and Chip were still in the room. They had been left behind. Three doors had opened. Wilf, Wilma, Kipper, Nadim and Neena had gone.

"I don't understand," cried Biff. "Why were we left behind?"

Mortlock shook his head. "You were not chosen," he said. "Now we must leave the task to the others and wait."

He pointed at the hourglass. The bright specks of light had already filled a quarter of the chamber.

"The others will soon be back," he explained. "In here, time is squeezed. What will seem like hours to them will pass here in moments."

"Are you sure the Circularium will work?" asked Chip anxiously.

"It will," said Mortlock, "but who has gone where, and whether they will succeed, I do not know. We can only wait and hope."

Biff looked at Chip. What on earth had they got themselves into?

Now what?

What other rooms might be behind the many doors in the Time Vault?

Why did Mortlock, the Time Guardian, pretend to be the school caretaker?

What is the TimeWeb and what will happen if the Virans get hold of it?

If Virans can look like ordinary people, how will the children recognise one?

Who has gone where and will they succeed?
Find out by reading any of the following:
The Jewel in the Hub, The Matrix Mission or The Power of the Cell.
... Every second is precious, so hurry!

Time Guardian

Is Mortlock human?
No. He is an ancient being, able to change his appearance and identity.

How many Time Guardians are there?
In the struggle to defeat the Virans, it seems only Mortlock is left.

Why doesn't Mortlock fight the Virans?
Too risky. He may be the last Time Guardian.

Why has he recruited Biff, Chip and the others?
To travel through time, an open, innocent mind is needed. Only children have this.

The TimeWeb

The TimeWeb is like a computer. The Hub is its hard drive, the Cell provides the power and the Matrix is its keyboard. It projects a huge glowing web of millions of tiny branch-like threads. If a Viran attacks somewhere, it'll be seen as a dark patch in the TimeWeb.

Mortlock has developed a programme which is able to see into the past. It sends images from history to a plasma globe. These images are often clues that help the children on their mission.

Glossary

ancient *(page 23)* Something that is very old. *"It is an ancient machine."*

exhibits *(page 8)* Items found in a public display or exhibition. Works of art, historical objects, etc. ... *a vast room full of exhibits on display.*

hourglass *(page 33)* Two connected glass containers, one above the other. It takes exactly an hour for the sand to drain from one container to the other. A way of measuring time. *In the centre of the room was a huge hourglass, almost as tall as Kipper.*

laboratory *(page 18)* A place where scientists use special equipment and carry out experiments. *Mortlock led them into a laboratory.*

symbols *(page 21)* Marks or signs that have a special meaning. *... they had a date on the spine with some strange letters and symbols.*

Thesaurus: Another word for ...

merge *(page 35)* mix, combine, blend, unite.

symbol *(page 21)* code, emblem, badge.

Have you read them all yet?

Level 11:

Level 12:

Time Runners	Mission Victory
Tyler: His Story	The Enigma Plot
A Jack and Three Queens	The Thief Who Stole Nothing

More great fiction from Oxford University Press:

www.winnie-the-witch.com

www.dinosaurcove.co.uk

About the Authors

Roderick Hunt MBE – creator of best-loved characters Biff, Chip, Kipper, Floppy and their friends. His first published stories were those he told his two sons at bedtime. Rod lives in Oxfordshire, in a house not unlike the house in the Magic Key adventures. In 2008, Roderick received an MBE for services to education, particularly literacy.

Roderick Hunt's son **David Hunt** was brought up on his father's stories and knows the world of Biff, Chip and Kipper intimately. His love of history and a good story has sparked many new ideas, resulting in the *Time Chronicles* series. David has had a successful career in the theatre, most recently working on scripts for Jude Law's *Hamlet* and *Henry V*, as well as Derek Jacobi's *Twelfth Night*.

Joint creator of the best-loved characters Biff, Chip, Kipper, Floppy and their friends, **Alex Brychta MBE** has brought each one to life with his fabulous illustrations, which are known and loved in many schools today. Following the Russian occupation of Czechoslovakia, Alex Brychta moved with his family from Prague to London. He studied graphic design and animation, before moving to the USA where he worked on animation for Sesame Street. Since then he has devoted many years of his career to *Oxford Reading Tree*, bringing detail, magic and humour to every story! In 2012 Alex received an MBE for services to children's literature.

Roderick Hunt and Alex Brychta won the prestigious Outstanding Achievement Award at the Education Resources Awards in 2009.

43

Levelling info for parents

What do the levels mean?

Read with Biff Chip & Kipper First Chapter Books have been designed by educational experts to help children develop as readers.

Each book is carefully levelled to allow children to make gradual progress and to feel confident and enjoy reading.

The Oxford Levels you will see on these books are used by teachers and are based on years of research in schools. Below is a summary of what each Oxford Level means, so that you can help your child to improve and enjoy their reading.

The books at Level 11 (Brown Book Band):

At this level, the sentence structures are becoming longer and more complex. The story plot may be more involved and there is a wider vocabulary. However, the proportion of unknown words used per paragraph/page is still carefully controlled to help build their reading stamina and allow children to read independently.

This level mostly covers characterisation through characters' actions and words rather than through description. The story may be organised in various ways, e.g. chronologically, thematically, sequentially, as relevant to the text type and subject.

The books at Level 12 (Grey Book Band):

At this level, the sentences are becoming more varied in structure and length. Though still straightforward, more inference may be required, e.g. in dialogue to work out who is speaking. Again, the story may be organised in various ways: chronologically, thematically, sequentially, etc., so that children can reflect on how the organisation helps the reader to understand the text.

The *Times Chronicles* books are also ideal for older children who feel less confident and need more practice in order to build stamina. The text is written to be age and ability appropriate, but also engaging, motivating and funny, making them a pleasure for children to read at this stage of their reading development.

OXFORD
UNIVERSITY PRESS

Great Clarendon Street, Oxford, OX2 6DP,
United Kingdom

Oxford University Press is a department of the University of Oxford.
It furthers the University's objective of excellence in research, scholarship,
and education by publishing worldwide. Oxford is a registered trade mark
of Oxford University Press in the UK and in certain other countries

Text written by David Hunt, based on the original characters created
by Roderick Hunt and Alex Brychta

First published 2010
This edition published in 2014

British Library Cataloguing in Publication Data
Data available

978-0-19-273906-3

1 3 5 7 9 10 8 6 4 2

Paper used in the production of this book is a natural, recyclable product
made from wood grown in sustainable forests. The manufacturing process
conforms to the environmental regulations of the country of origin.

Printed in China

Acknowledgements
The publisher and authors would like to thank the following for their
permission to reproduce photographs and other copyright material:
end papers: Omela/Shutterstock; Iguasu/Shutterstock; Eric Gevaert/
Shutterstock; Mikhail/Shutterstock; Leigh Prather/Shutterstock

Book quiz answers
1 b
2 Dark energy
3 He turns the hourglass upside down.